Heart of Stone:

A Paranormal Protector Tale

A tale in the Heart of Stone series

DEMELZA CARLTON

ONE

For weeks now, Ben had been able to focus on nothing else but escape. Escape from that stone prison. He might only have a hammer and chisel, but by all he held dear, he was going to break free…

"For a moment there, it looked like you were a gargoyle – you lined up so perfectly with those wings and horns, I could have sworn you were the demon…oh, just like that! If you could only see your face…" Torstan doubled over with laughter.

Ben set down his tools and glanced over his shoulder. Yes, the first gargoyle looked lifelike enough, its wings arched out as if ready to leap into flight, but this second one eluded him. It was almost as though the creature didn't want to be released from its stone prison. It had to be, though, because Sir William Burke wanted two gargoyles on this folly, and it would not be complete without them. And if they didn't complete the job, they'd never earn enough to pay for their passage to the Colonies, and they'd be stuck as penniless crofters here for the rest of their lives.

"Maybe I should carve a likeness of your face into this gargoyle," Ben said, but even as the words left his lips, he knew he wouldn't. This gargoyle continued to elude him. Maybe this piece of limestone held a trapped, beautiful woman instead, a statue of some long-lost warrior queen…

No. This stone block held a gargoyle of some sort. He just had to know what it looked like, see the image in his head that lay in the stone, and he'd be able to chip away at it until he'd freed the creature.

And he and Torstan could go free. Landholders, farmers in their own right, not beholden to any knight or lord who was no better a man than any of the

Stone brothers, no matter what they pretended. Where all men were free and equal…

Torstan dusted off his hands. "As long as it's hideous enough to please Sir William, carve whatever face you want into it. Now that I think of it, though…that first one does look a lot like Dunstan. That narrow eyed look he'd get, just before he was about to give us a roasting about whatever mischief we'd managed to get into while he was helping Father on the farm."

Ben squinted at the gargoyle. "That afternoon we came home early from school and you decided the apples were ready for harvest, though it was far too early…I believed you, and we picked a bushel before I bit into one and discovered you were wrong…that's the expression he had on his face that day. Like a demon come to drag us both down to eternal damnation."

Torstan sighed. "Oh, what I'd give for one of those apples now. As it is, we should sail before they're ripe this year. If we ever get this job finished."

Ben managed a smile. "We will. And we'll write to Dunstan, to tell him where he might find us at the new Stone Farm, so when he's done sailing, he can settle down to farming with us."

"Yes, yes, but there won't be a Stone Farm until we're finished with this folly. You have gargoyles to carve, I have walls to build, and there's only so many hours in the day. Get to it!"

Ben did his best approximation of a

courtly bow, like he imagined the lords in London did to girls they fancied at a ball. "Yes, m'lord Torstan. At once!"

For a moment, laughter rose up from the construction site, before it was replaced by the clink and clunk of hammer on chisel, and stone on stone. After all, picturesque castle ruins did not build themselves.

TWO

Dunstan squinted at the shore suspiciously. After so much time at sea, so many foreign ports, he wasn't sure if he was dreaming, or if this was really home.

"Me and some of the boys are going ashore. Are you coming? The waterfront taverns are all well and good for those that don't know, but there's an inn on the far side of town that serves the best dark ale in the country. Maybe even the world."

Dunstan nodded. "The New Inn." Though it hadn't been new for centuries, and he'd never managed to discover what happened to the old inn, if it had ever existed at all. "Will there be time for even a pint of ale? The last time we went drinking at a proper pub, I never saw so much of a sip of ale, before the captain had us out of there, ready to load his new cargo so we could leave in the morning."

"Ah, no chance of that! We'll be ashore for a couple of weeks, maybe more, this time." Johnson winked.

Uneasiness churned in Dunstan's belly. Captain Cammell did not hold with ships sitting idle in port. There'd have to be a compelling reason for him to stay here for so long. "What have you heard that I haven't?"

Johnson puffed out his chest. "I heard that we've been hired by no less than the Secretary of the Colonies, to bring passengers and supplies to the brand new Swan River Colony."

The Swan River Colony was twenty years old if it was a day – and his uncle had been waiting for Dunstan and his brothers to join him there since the Colony first opened. Perhaps this was his chance to buy passage for all of them. Or, better yet, earn their passage by working during the voyage, and use the precious coin he'd saved to buy what they'd need to start farming the moment they landed. The more equipment they brought with them, the more land the Governor would grant them. Then they'd be their own masters, answering to no one but each other, a far cry from their life as crofters here.

Two weeks would be more than enough time to head home, persuade his brothers, and bring them back here, ready to head for the Colony. Perhaps the captain would allow him to leave tonight, if he caught him in time.

As if fate was on his side for once, Captain Cammell appeared before him.

No time like the present.

"Evening, Captain," Dunstan began.

THREE

Sun streaming through Pamela's window woke her. It was watery, but sunlight nevertheless, and the first fine day in weeks. She had no intention of wasting a moment of this good weather. She was dressed and headed downstairs in a trice, her satchel of drawing things bumping against her hip on every step.

Gone were the days when a maid had brought her breakfast and helped her dress. Now Mrs Jewkes was the only servant they could afford, and she was so busy doing double duty as both cook and housekeeper, Pamela didn't dare ask her to do any more.

"You're up early, Miss Pamela," Mrs Jewkes said, pulling the bread from the oven and laying it on the table.

"The morning light is so lovely for sketching today," Pamela replied. She'd planned to take something cold from the larder for breakfast, but the smell of fresh baked bread tempted her worse than the devil himself.

"I'll pack you a basket of breakfast to take with you, then. Your father was up late last night, and not likely to wake before noon, so he'll likely not want a hot meal before dinnertime," Mrs Jewkes said.

Father had been drinking again, and would be sleeping off his hangover for many hours yet, was what the housekeeper did not say, though it hung in the air between them all the same. They both knew he'd done the same every night since he'd returned from London. Before he'd left, he'd talked of changing their fortunes, so that maybe Pamela might accompany him on his next trip and she'd get to enjoy a season of balls and parties. But after his return, he'd not talked of anything, and Pamela feared that meant their fortunes had only changed for the worse.

Perhaps fate would smile on her instead, and help her find a rich husband who might change her fortunes, and hence her father's, too. Though how she was supposed to meet such a man here in Burke Castle, she had no idea. With only Mrs Jewkes, they could hardly entertain on the sort of grand scale that would throw a duke or perhaps a lord her way.

Though they'd likely be old or cruel or have some other failing that made them horrible husbands, or some duke's daughter would have snapped them up long ago. Still, if there were something Pamela could do so that her father might smile again, instead of sitting silently every night, drinking himself into an early grave, she would endure almost anything.

"Are you well, Miss Pamela?"

Pamela blinked. While she'd been wool-gathering, Mrs Jewkes had packed her basket and now held it out expectantly. "Yes, just lost in my thoughts. Wondering where I should go to draw today." Perhaps down by the old quarry, where the water-filled pit reflected the blue sky and surrounding hills. Best that she take the cliff path to get there, so she could see if any rainclouds threatened to send her home early. Unless she could see clear to the isles, in which case she might sketch the seascape instead. "Do you think…"

But Mrs Jewkes was already hard at work on the other side of the kitchen, no longer paying any attention to Pamela.

Pamela huffed out a little laugh. If she were some fine lady to a far finer castle, she'd likely take umbrage at being ignored by a servant, but Burke Castle had long lost any finery it might once have had in the centuries it had stood on the sea cliffs, and if Mrs Jewkes saw fit to leave the castle, Pamela herself would take her place in the kitchens. A frightening prospect that would likely result in her poisoning her father and herself, for the only feminine arts Pamela possessed were for drawing and painting, not cookery.

Father had brought her a new sketchbook and pastels from London. Perhaps if she sketched something pretty with them, she might make him smile again. Heavens knew nothing else she'd tried had worked.

The colours would be brighter by the quarry, she decided, so that's where she went. Except, when she crested the last hill, she found no watery mirror waiting for her. Instead, the place was a veritable ants' nest of activity, with half a dozen men cutting and hauling blocks of dusty white stone.

"What's going on? Where are you taking these?" she demanded.

The men glanced at each other, before one stepped forward. "Up to the masons, miss." He pointed at the next hill, where she'd planned to sit and sketch.

She squinted up at it. Something was taking shape up there, though it was too low to be sure what.

Could it be a new house, something more modern than crumbling Burke Castle? Perhaps Father's luck had changed for the better while he was in London, and he'd wanted to surprise her.

Well, colour her surprised – now she'd seen the start of it, she had to see how the work progressed. She trudged past the quarry and up the next hill.

FOUR

It wasn't until she'd crested the hill that Pamela could see any of what they were building. It looked like a smaller version of Burke Castle, only with it being built on the windward side of the hill, looking out to sea, it would likely be colder and even more draughty than the original. Hardly an improvement. What was her father thinking?

A man appeared from behind the wall, pushing a stone into place.

"You there!" she said, striding toward him. "What are you building."

"It's a folly, miss."

She laughed. "That it is. Who'd want to live somewhere so windy?"

The man's brow creased. "No, it's a folly, miss. Sir William Burke commissioned us to build a folly, a picturesque ruined castle here, complete with statues and the like. Something that can be seen from the upper levels of the north side of Burke Castle, when Sir William is gazing toward the sea, he said."

Ah, that was why she hadn't seen it.

Her windows faced south, and the other rooms in the castle she frequented were all on the ground floor. The upper storeys on the north side of the castle were her father's rooms, and the ball room, a vast space filled with cloth-shrouded furnishings, ghosts from a past that would never come to light again. It had been so for all of Pamela's lifetime, and likely for most of her father's, too, for she'd heard Father say that the gambling debts her grandfather had amassed in his youth had meant they had no luxuries like balls, or any such entertainments.

Yet in a better world, when the moon was full, one might leave the whirl of dancers in the ballroom to stand upon the terrace, and wonder at the ruin on the last hill before the sea, silhouetted in the moonlight, a mystery to haunt the eye and one's dreams for many a night after the ball was done. In fact, she could see it so clearly, she wanted to set it down on paper, a stark rendering in charcoal on the white page…

She wandered down the hill a little, until when she looked up, the stone walls stretched up into the sky from the hilltop. If she but imagined the moon where the sun now stood, its brilliant rays heralding its imminent rise above the jagged top of the half-constructed tower…

Pamela lost herself in her picture, and her perfect moment where there was nothing but her and the sky, the hilltop and the stones casting their shadow over the valley below.

FIVE

"More stone, Mr Stone," said a respectful voice.

Ben glanced up. Torstan was nowhere to be seen and Dunstan's demonic effigy was unable to speak, so the men with the cart appeared to be speaking to him.

"I'm just Ben, lads, a former farmer's

son just trying to make a living, same as you," Ben said.

He recognised the stony look on their faces, and sighed inwardly. He'd only grown up two villages away from theirs, but it might as well have been a world away, for they were strangers. And if they were cutting stone in the quarry, while he and his brother carved it and constructed a castle, that made him a cut above them. Damn the English landlords and their infernal social classes. All the more reason to move to the Colonies, where all men were created equal, or so some said.

"Where would you like us to put it, Mr Stone?"

Ben opened his mouth to tell them to put it with the rest, but he blinked at the empty space where there had been stone blocks the last time he'd looked. Torstan must have incorporated them into the castle already. He'd best leave Dunstan's statue and get started on the next one, or Torstan would finish the castle before the decorations were done.

"Just…there," he said, waving at the empty patch of ground. He watched the men unload block after block, until one caught his eye. Not cut as straight as the rest, there was a slight natural curve in the stone, almost as if…

"Except that one. Bring that one here," he commanded.

"It wasn't broken when we loaded it onto the cart, Mr Stone. I don't know what happened. Maybe there was a fault in the stone and somehow it broke as we came up the hill. I'll bring more stone up directly to replace it…" The man continued, twisting his cap in his hands, but Ben wasn't listening.

The damaged block landed at his feet and Ben circled it, predatory as a cat. A section of the stone had sheared off along some ancient fault line, curving and undulating like the hills around him, or so he'd thought at first. Now, up close, it looked more like a woman's curves, curled up on her side as if asleep. He could only see the barest hint now – her face was hidden within the intact block, and he yearned to release her. To wake her from her endless slumber.

He lifted his hammer and chisel, holding his breath as he chipped off the tiniest piece. Then another.

"No, that's not right," a distinctly feminine voice said.

Ben blinked. Surely the stone could not have spoken to him? He squinted at the chips he'd chiselled off, at precisely the moment in which the sun chose to make a rare appearance. The creamy coloured stone caught the light, turning the trapped woman into a blinding beacon that shone brighter than the sun itself. Ben shook his head, determined to restore his vision. He could not carve what he could not see.

Only then did he see her, and only because she moved. Her gown and bonnet were green as the grass on the hill behind her, only a few shades lighter than the cloth-covered book in her hands. She lifted it to shade her eyes, as she glared crossly at the sun.

Ben laughed aloud. At first, he'd thought her fey, or some other sort of supernatural creature, there one moment, and gone in a blink, but only a human woman would rail at the sun so for spoiling her light. And one of the quality, no doubt, for who but a lady, who'd never known a day of hardship in her life, would rail at the sun in the sky simply for shining?

Luckily, she hadn't heard or noticed him. That was for the best, Ben suspected, for a woman who felt herself superior to the sun would likely be even more cross if some common farm boy or apprentice mason were to enter her field of view and spoil her sketch.

For that was what she was doing in the

book, her hand moving in swift, sure strokes that made Ben's own hand itch to do the same.

When the workday was done, he promised himself. His sketchbook was nowhere near as fine as the green lady's, and he had naught but charcoal to draw with, but he was fortunate enough to have drawing tools in the cottage he and his brother shared, and perhaps an hour's leisure time in the long summer evenings in which he might indulge in a sketch or two. He should try drawing the sleeping woman in the stone, to help him with his carving tomorrow, but it was the green lady who stayed in his thoughts more than anyone else.

Ben had to force himself to return to the work at hand, the white woman instead of the green one. Her arms soon held him in her thrall. One curled around, bent at the elbow, with her hand cradling her head, but the other she'd flung out in front of her, almost reaching for something out of sight. Or perhaps protecting…what?

The sun beat down on Ben and his stone, but he was oblivious to anything but the tap of hammer and chisel as he slowly, painstakingly released the slumbering woman from her prison.

SIX

Pamela shook her head. She was too old for such childish fancies. Nothing fearful lurked in the dark and shadows were no more than a trick of the light. If she fancied a monster to sketch, there was a stone one halfway down the hill, a winged demon whose face resembled the man she'd spoken to in the ruins. He must be a hard master indeed if his apprentice had carved his likeness into a demon. Until the carver appeared, and she saw that he was older than most apprentices. The way the workmen spoke to him, calling him "Mr Stone", spoke of more respect than an apprentice could command. And the skill in his work…

Pamela watched, fascinated, as the damaged stone block the workers had dropped at the demon's feet began to take shape under the man's hammer and chisel. It looked like a child's knee…no, an elbow, and a second arm, stretched out over something, the fingers curling around it protectively. Pamela smiled. She wouldn't trust that winged demon with her treasures, either.

She took up a pencil and began to draw again, capturing the demon's beetled brow and the shadows thrown across its face by the rising sun. Then the man kneeling at his feet, chipping away at those two stone arms, as if he intended to pull the arms' owner from the stone's grasp and save her from the demon. For surely it was a woman.

The sun beat down, but Pamela was oblivious to it. The man shrugged out of his shirt, hanging it over the demon as though the creature had been nothing but a clothes horse, before returning to his carving.

Never had Pamela's hands moved so fast across the page, sketching the man and his work, the demon and his shirt, every movement presenting a new angle her eye wished captured forever.

The sun disappeared behind the clouds again, and the demon lost his shirt, but not before she'd seen the man throw his head back as he gulped down some water, the muscles in his neck and chest moving like they had a life of their own. That the simple act of drinking could appear so perfect, so powerful…

Her pencil flew across the page, striving to capture the movement in a single picture. She'd drawn six, the last with water streaming down the man's chest as he'd spilled some, and when she looked at it, she felt the most peculiar fluttering in her belly, as though she'd swallowed a butterfly. Such a strange sensation.

Pamela forced herself to look away. To stare at the dark, cold stone atop the hill, to the bones of a castle that would never be whole, crumbling walls that would only ever know emptiness, for they would never support a roof that made the place a home. There was no history to this place, no battles fought, no darkness or light to give it life. It was simply…grey, reflecting the skies above.

She turned to a new page, and set to work anew, but with a pencil and not charcoal this time. Ah, that was more like it. The lines no longer wavered, wanting to show what wasn't there instead of what was.

Pamela was almost done sketching the construction, and debating whether to include the clouds behind it, when the sun dipped below the clouds on its evening dive into the sea, lighting the folly on fire.

The fresh cut stone glowed gold, haloed by the clouds that had crowded in like dark memories only a moment before.

Pamela couldn't seem to close her mouth. She wanted, no, she needed to capture the colours. Now, before they faded. She dug through her satchel for her pastels, and feverishly began to add colour to the drab drawing.

It seemed only a moment or two, but it could have been an hour, when the light faded and the castle ruin returned to greyness once more. Pamela sagged, letting the pastel box fall to the grass. She cradled her sketchbook in her lap, breathless at the bright colours she'd seen and captured on the page, but twilight threatened to leach away those vibrant colours if she didn't make it home before dark. She might even get lost, for she had not thought to bring a lantern to light her way.

Reluctantly, she packed everything back into her satchel, scooped up the basket that had somehow emptied itself during the day – she had no memory of eating a single bite, but she must have – and headed home.

But even as she bent her steps toward Burke Castle, her heart and mind remained in the ruins, stealing a whispered promise that she would return on the morrow.

SEVEN

By the time the sun rose, Dunstan heartily wished he'd stopped for a drink and a meal at the New Inn, or, better yet, a bed for the night. His feet were sore from walking so far, and he longed to break his fast, but when he reached the Thieving Kelpie, the tavern a little over a mile from the cottage his brothers called home, was locked up tight, not yet open.

His brothers would have breakfast for him, he consoled himself, as he trudged on. And while the innkeeper and his staff would not thank him for an early waking, his brothers would certainly be happy to see him.

Smoke already rose from the chimneys of the crofters' cottages, though his brothers had yet to light their morning fire. Perhaps they were still abed. Then again, in this warm summer weather, maybe they took their breakfast cold.

Dunstan rapped smartly on the door, then waited. After a long moment with no response, he knocked again.

The door at the next cottage swung open, and John McLeod peered out.

"Who's that?" he demanded.

"Dunstan Stone, on shore leave, come to visit my brothers," Dunstan replied. Had he changed so much that MacLeod didn't recognise him? MacLeod himself was thinner and more wrinkled than Dunstan remembered him, with more grey than brown in his hair.

"Young Dunstan, is it? It's been an age since I saw you, boy." McLeod scrutinised him. "The sea suits you, more than carpentering ever did."

Dunstan opened his mouth to tell the man he was a ship's carpenter, working with wood on the sea just as much as he ever did ashore, then thought the better of it and closed his mouth again. McLeod, like many of their neighbours, was born and would die a crofter, with farming so deeply ingrained in his blood it was a wonder he didn't bleed black like the rich soil he tilled. McLeod would sooner die than leave his homeland for the wilds of Australia. Or take up a trade like carpentry.

"If you're here to see your brothers, you're too late. They've been gone several sennights or more."

"Gone? Gone where?" They couldn't have left for the Swan River Colony without him. At least, not without leaving a note. Perhaps they'd sent him a letter that was even now awaiting him on the *Scindian*.

"Building some English lord's castle, down by the coast, or so he said. Your brother Torstan's a master mason now, a proper builder, with young Ben as his apprentice," MacLeod said proudly, for all the world as if he was their father. "Apparently, Lord Burke requested them especially."

Dunstan's heart sank. If his brothers were building a castle, it might be years before it was finished — they'd never be able to sail with the *Scindian*. "Then I'd best be getting down to Burke Castle. Thanks for the direction, MacLeod," he said, forcing out a smile.

Longing for a rest, but knowing he could not take the time, Dunstan headed back into the village, toward the coast road.

Smoke rose from the chimneys of the Thieving Kelpie now, and a familiar figure stood outside, shaking a rug so forcefully, Dunstan suspected it was due for a sound beating.

"Cara Raeburn! Just the lass I've been longing to see!" he exclaimed.

She turned, and his breath caught in his throat as he anticipated seeing her beautiful face and figure for the first time in far too long.

"Why, if it isn't Dun Stone. Have you come looking for your brothers? For you won't find them here. Harvests were too poor these last three years, they went looking for work along the coast. Building for the English, or so I've heard," she said, folding her arms around the rug.

Dunstan drank her in, like a marooned man who'd found his first freshwater stream on foreign soil. Not a day at sea had gone by without him imagining her as his wife, sailing away to the Colony together, to start their new life. "Come with me to the Swan River Colony, Cara, as my wife," he breathed.

She made a derisive sound deep in her throat. "What, and leave Oscar and the Kelpie? You're daft, Dun Stone, if you think I'm going out to the Colonies like some convict, when I have a comfortable life here!"

"Oscar…Oscar Baldwin?" He'd been Dunstan's best friend as a boy, when they'd been at school together, before Dunstan had been apprenticed to a shipyard and Oscar had taken over his father's farm. Dunstan hadn't seen him in years. "Is he here?"

"Of course, you fool. He's fast asleep, seeing as he worked the bar late last

night, so you keep your voice down —
don't want him waking yet. He's a right
bear when he hasn't had enough sleep,
and no mistake."

One of the maids hurried out and
dropped a curtsey in front of Cara. "If
you please, Mrs Baldwin, one of the
guests has taken ill. Wants me to call the
doctor. Shall I fetch him, ma'am?"

While Cara made enquiries about how
much the man had had to drink the night
before, and how much coin he carried,
Dunstan heard none of it. Two words
had gotten their teeth into his mind, and
would not let go. *Mrs Baldwin.*

"Hang on. You married Oscar?" he
demanded.

He prayed he'd heard wrong. That it
wasn't so. He'd been in love with Cara

forever, wanted her to be his wife, and she'd even agreed to it, that night up in the hayloft, when she'd given her body to him, just before he joined the *Scindian*.

"Of course I did. A baby must have a father, and you weren't anywhere to be found," she snapped. Her eyes blazed. "Oscar's a good father to his son, and he'll be a good father to this one, too." She patted her belly through her skirts. Only now did Dunstan realise that the rug had hidden her advanced pregnancy.

She'd gotten pregnant from that night in the hayloft? He had a son. "Cara…"

"It's Mrs Baldwin to you. I'm a respectable married woman and mother," she snapped.

"But I thought…"

"No, Dun Stone, you didn't think.

And what you did think, you thought wrong. Be gone with you — we don't want you here," she said, shooing him away. "Get yourself gone, Dun, before I call the grooms to chase you off. Go to the Colonies, with all the convicts, and good riddance."

Dunstan fancied he heard the crack of his heart shattering into a million pieces as he turned his back on Cara and forced himself to head, once more, for the sea.

EIGHT

While Torstan fetched their dinner from the inn in the village, Ben sat on the bench outside their cottage and tried to draw the sleeping stone woman. Her arms and hands, and the curve of her torso as she curled onto her side to sleep, he could draw with his eyes closed, for they were plain to see, already sculpted in stone. But her face, and her legs, and even what garments she wore, if any, were a mystery to him.

He might not know what she was wearing, but he certainly knew she wasn't wearing that bell-like skirt the green woman had worn today. He sketched the lines of it, the swell of her breast and the curve of her neck as she'd sketched the castle with such fierce concentration. And that wicked smile she'd worn, like the cat stealing the cream from the dairy, triumphant at her own daring. If her face had made such a striking picture, how had her drawing compared? He longed to know, but hadn't dared ask.

Perhaps if she returned tomorrow…

Yes, he told himself, he would

summon all his courage and ask to see her sketchbook. After all, she was a fine lady, with better tools for her art than he'd ever possessed, with likely the benefits of a proper education to improve her drawing from the sort of rough sketches he still did. Her work was sure to be exquisite, the best he'd ever seen.

If she returned.

In fact, she did return, and he spent the whole day in an agony of uncertainty, debating what to do. He knew that because she was one of the quality, good manners dictated that it was up to her to introduce herself, or at least be the first to acknowledge him, and not the other way around. But the traitorous part of his mind kept throwing up other possibilities. She was shy. She did not know it was her place to speak first. She'd taken a terrible oath never to speak to a man. Or she simply had no desire to speak to him because he was so far beneath her notice.

He knew this last was most likely to be true, but day after day, he felt her eyes on him as he slowly drew the slumbering lady out of her stone prison. Finally, he made a bargain with himself. If the Lady Artist (for she did not wear green every day, so she was no longer the green lady in his mind) did not speak to him before the statue was done, then he would take the first step and introduce himself.

So, on the day he finished smoothing the statue's back, he set down his tools, swallowed, and lifted his head.

She had her eyes fixed on him already, or perhaps it was the statue, and Ben made up his mind.

"Does she meet with milady's approval?" Ben asked, relieved to hear he'd managed to keep the shake of trepidation confined to his belly and out of his voice.

She dropped her pencil in surprise. "I…I'm sure I could not say."

Perhaps she was shy after all. Ben grew bolder. "Then come down and take a closer look for yourself. The approval of such an accomplished artist would be a great compliment, I'm sure." Not that he'd seen her art, but he was certain it had to be better than anything he could create.

She rose obediently, dusting off her

skirts as she approached with slow, measured steps. She stopped a yard away from the statue, taking it in, before circling it, like a nervous young predator stalking its first prey. As if she'd somehow heard his thoughts, comparing her to a beast, her cheeks flushed pink.

"She's…well, she's not wearing very much, is she?"

Now it was Ben's turn to blush. He'd intended to put a night rail on the woman, or some sort of dress, but the stone had shaped itself beneath his chisel, forming the smooth lines of a woman's skin, wound only in a sheet. Even her hair hung free, unbound curls cascading down her back and across one shoulder, hiding most of her breast. She might be naked in her slumber, but the statue was still a most modest young miss. "In the privacy of her bedchamber, perhaps she has fallen asleep while waiting for her husband," Ben suggested.

The lady's face grew redder still. "Do women…wives…actually do that?"

Ben laughed. "Do what? Sleep?"

"No. Lie naked in bed for their husbands."

Ben's mouth grew suddenly dry. "I…would not know. I'm not married, and nor is my brother." Though he would like to be, one day. "Have you never fallen asleep while waiting for your husband?"

"I'm…I…I have fallen asleep many a time, and yes, perhaps I am waiting, but…I do not have a husband, nor any prospects, and I can scarcely imagine lying in bed, nude…before I am…why, the very idea is preposterous!"

She was a fine lady indeed, who had never been too poor to afford nightclothes. But to tell her that many people slept naked out of necessity would only add to her horror. He had no desire to drive her away.

"So is waking a sleeping woman or a winged demon from stone, and yet it all in a day's work for me," Ben said. "Ben Stone, apprentice stonemason, and occasional sculptor." He ducked his head.

"Aren't you a bit old to be an apprentice?" she asked.

Torstan had said the same thing, many a time. "In truth, yes, but my brother tells me if I only spent more time building walls and not carving statues, I'd be a master mason within a year. I can work stone well enough, but every time I try to build a wall, I'll get distracted by one of the blocks and…" He gestured at the sleeping statue. "She had no desire to be trapped in a wall. She wanted to be free."

The lady frowned. "She does not look free to me. Look, the way her hand stretches out, as if she fell asleep, exhausted, from begging to be set free."

Ben stared at the statue, trying to see it as the lady did. No matter how long he stared, he couldn't. "That arm rests protectively atop her books, milady. See how her fingers curl around the spine of this one? She does not want to let go, even in sleep."

"I'm sure I know of no woman who would choose books over clothing of any kind, Mr Stone. She is a fanciful creation of your own, to be sure. A creature of myth."

"She is no less real or fanciful than the demon who keeps watch over her, milady," Ben said, gesturing at the gargoyle.

The lady shook her head. "I'm not…not a lady. I'm just…Pamela. Pamela Burke. And unless I have the good fortune to marry a man with a title, that's all I shall ever be."

Ben bowed, hoping he was doing things right. "I'm honoured to make your acquaintance, Miss Burke. Ah…are you a relation of Sir William Burke, our current employer?"

She ducked her head. "He's my father. Though I can't imagine him paying you to carve a naked woman for him."

Ben felt the heat rising in his cheeks again. "He didn't, milady…uh, Miss Burke. He did commission two gargoyles, to go with the picturesque ruin. He wanted them up on the tower my brother's building now. The lady was…the stone was broken, and I saw…I saw a lady trapped in the stone, and I had no choice but to release her." It sounded like madness.

Yet Miss Burke only smiled. "When I first tried to draw the castle, I could not see it for what it was, but for what it might be. My first sketches are all of a complete castle, reaching high into the sky, where a whole household of lords and ladies, knights and squires, might have defended the coast against raiders from the north in centuries gone by. I did not see the picturesque as I am supposed to."

"May I see?" Ben asked eagerly, reaching for her sketchbook.

Miss Burke clasped the book to her breast, as protective as her slumbering stone sister. "I have never…not since Father sent my governess away…no one has seen my drawings."

Just as no one had ever seen her sleep naked, Ben guessed. He sighed. He'd gone too far, as he always did when talking about art. Miss Burke would complain to her father, who would take one look at the nude woman and likely throw both him and his brother off his estate, without paying them a penny for all the work they'd already done. They'd never reach the Swan River Colony, and it would be all his fault.

He swallowed. He had to make this right. He bowed low, so low he feared he'd fall over if he didn't keep this short. "My apologies, Miss Burke. I did not mean to offend. I'm just a simple farm boy, who has a small amount of skill working stone. I know little of art, or fine things."

He turned on his heel to return to his work.

"Mr Stone…Ben…please, wait."

NINE

"May I see?"

Pamela longed to hand him her sketchbook, in the fervent hope that Mr Stone might see something in her work to give her hope to continue. She knew she'd never have the kind of skill to create a perfect likeness that seemed about to step off the page and speak, as he had with his sleeping woman statue, but if she could paint or sketch something good enough to go in a gallery, then she might find some rich patron who would help her, take her away from Burke Castle and introduce her into society.

But if Mr Stone saw her pictures and did not like them, he might dash her hopes with a single look. Worse, if he looked at the fanciful castles she'd drawn on that first day, he might think her mad, as her governess had when she'd seen Pamela's pictures of Miss Smith as a witch. She'd never seen Miss Smith cast a spell, eat a toad, wear a pointed hat or fly through the air upon a broom, but it didn't take much imagination for Pamela to believe it of her strict governess, for the woman was positively diabolical. An opinion Miss Smith had only reinforced when she'd thrust Pamela's sketchbook into the nursery fire, spanked her soundly, then threatened her with more of the same if she ever dared to draw again.

Father's fortunes had failed soon after that, and Miss Smith had been dismissed from her post because education was something her father could no longer afford, but it had been several years before Pamela had dared to take up a pencil again.

And yet, here was Mr Stone, a master artist if ever she saw one, asking to see her sketches. No, turning away from her, while she stood there wool-gathering.

No, she could not let this opportunity pass. If Mr Stone told her that her drawings were terrible, she would never sketch again.

Pamela wet her lips. "Mr Stone!"

He did not turn.

She took a deep breath. Dare she? "Ben? Please, wait."

Mr Stone turned, and she was surprised to find no censure in his eyes at her daring to use his given name. "I am at your service, Miss Burke."

She thrust out the book. "Please. If you'd…be so kind as to take a look. Perhaps you can tell me how I might improve." As long as he didn't demand she bare her buttocks for a whipping, anything he said could not hurt as much as Miss Smith's criticism.

She kept her eyes on the statue as she felt Mr Stone take the book from her hands. The decidedly nude statue. A sheet covered much of her front, but her buttocks were clear to be seen, bare to the sky. Mr Stone must have seen many naked woman to craft one so true to life. And what woman would refuse a man who could immortalise what he saw in stone? To have people stare up at her image for centuries, falling in love with a statue they could only admire from afar, long after she had departed this life. Heaven help her, but if Mr Stone asked, she would not refuse such an offer. It was a chance at immortality.

Not to mention, she'd seen the way Mr Stone looked at the stone woman as he'd carved her. Every stroke like a lover, his gaze hungry as his hands roamed her body. What had he called it? Freeing her from her prison, he'd said. Pamela only wished he'd take those strong hands and free her next.

"Miss Burke?"

Pamela pressed her hands to her heated cheeks, hoping to cool them, but they only seemed to grow hotter still. "Yes, Mr Stone?"

"Your castle looks like something that belongs in a gothic novel. I beg your pardon if that offends you, but it looks so dark and forbidding. The coloured drawing, here, is much warmer, with a great deal more detail, and if you had not said, I would not have believed you were sketching the same structure. This would not be out of place on your drawing room wall."

Pamela started to stammer out her thanks, but Mr Stone cut her off with a wave of his hand.

"It is these, however, where your talent truly shines. I have never seen such lifelike renditions of the human form. Did you study under an Italian master, by any chance?"

Pamela burst out laughing. "Heavens, no! I've never met an Italian, let alone studied with one. Father had some books with pictures of Italian paintings, though. I would give anything to visit Italy and see the real thing. Have you been to Italy, Mr Stone?"

He shook his head. "One day, perhaps, but not yet. You should ask your father to take you."

It was Pamela's turn to shake her head. "My father would never agree to take me to Italy. I've never been more than ten miles from home, and as I'm Father's heir, I likely never will go further than that. Father says there is no need for a girl to be educated in anything beyond being a good and biddable wife. I will never see Italy, outside of dreams."

He handed back her book. "Then if you'll forgive my impertinence, Miss Burke, your father is a fool. Talent like yours should be nurtured, and not allowed to die. If you truly wish to go to Italy and study with the masters there, as you should, you will find a way."

He was a man. He couldn't possibly understand. "So do you not truly wish for that, Mr Stone? For if you have not been to Italy, then you have not found a way. And if you cannot, I don't see how you think I have any hope of doing so."

He spread his arms wide. "Miss Burke, my father was a farmer. I am but an apprentice mason. Yet this is my way, or at least I hope it is. My brothers and I are working hard to earn the money to pay for our passage to the Colonies, specifically the Swan River Colony, where we mean to make our fortunes. Then, before too long, I hope to have the funds to travel to Italy."

From the way his dreamy eyes shone, she knew he intended to do exactly that. Whatever it took, however hard he had to work, Ben Stone would see Italy. Pamela sighed. "I would give everything I own to go with you."

Mr Stone grinned. "If that's truly what you wish, then I don't doubt you will."

But…an unaccompanied girl could not travel with a bachelor like Mr Stone. It simply wasn't proper. "My father would never permit it," she said sadly.

He leaned in. "Your father will not live forever, Miss Burke. And you will not live at all unless you believe at least some of your dreams can come true."

"Ben, come home, it's time for dinner." The older Mr Stone, the one who was building the castle ruins, stood above them, frowning at them. "You should not be bothering Miss Burke."

Pamela opened her mouth to say that Ben was not bothering her at all. Quite the opposite, in fact. She wished she'd spoken to him sooner.

Except that Ben bowed and hurried off to obey his brother's summons before she could get a word out.

Pamela sighed. She'd best head home for dinner, too. Her mind was whirling with possibilities. Well, impossibilities, which might become possible, if she could but find a way.

She'd return tomorrow, as, she was certain, would Ben.

TEN

"Have you tied it securely?" Torstan asked for what Ben thought must be the hundredth time.

"YES!" Ben shouted back.

"Are you sure?"

"YES!"

"Then start lifting it…careful now…"

Torstan had managed the winch fine on his own until now, but now the tower walls were too high to reach without a ladder, and the only way to build them higher still was to have one man atop the ladder with another manning the winch. So Ben had downed his tools, leaving the second gargoyle in its barely touched block of stone, and come up to help Torstan.

"Look out!"

Ben threw his body sideways only a moment before the block he'd been hoisting crashed to the ground where his feet had been.

"Ben, you fool! You didn't tie the knots securely enough and it slipped out. That's the second time! Get your head out of the clouds and back down to earth, or we'll never get the job done!"

Ben wanted to protest that his thoughts had been on Miss Pamela, who watched them avidly as she sketched their progress. Yesterday, she'd brought one of her precious Italian art books, full of religious paintings of heaven, hell and everything in between, rendered in glorious colour plates. But he didn't dare mention her name. Torstan had told him to stay away from her, and not speak to her at all, but when she came to him, so eager to converse, Ben had not the heart to refuse her. He'd never been able to discuss art with anyone, and she had such a keen eye! Why, she'd spotted the tiniest details in those Italian paintings that he hadn't even noticed until she pointed them out. He longed to head down the hill to her side, instead of heaving rocks about on ropes until his arms ached.

Knots and ropes put him in mind of Dunstan.

"If Dunstan was here, you'd have no worry about the knots, or the ropes. I wish he'd come home," Ben blurted out.

"Aye, so do I, but he's off sailing the seas, earning his own fare to the Colony, while we toil away here. Once this job is finished, we'll have enough coin to pay our passage. Then, the next walls we build will be the farmhouse at our new home." Torstan closed his eyes for a moment, as though imagining what that house might look like. Then he fixed his gaze on Ben once more. "And if you drop any of the stones for our house, there'll be hell to pay, I promise you."

Ben nodded. "Of course not. It'll be our home. Every stone hand cut from Swan River limestone. I'll even carve you a gargoyle or three to protect the place when we're not home."

Torstan shook his head. "Don't be silly. Gargoyles are for castles and cathedrals and other such grand places, not our cottage. And you're still a gargoyle short on this castle, so you'd best head back down that hill and get to work on it, or we won't finish on time and Sir William will be cross."

Worse, he might dock their pay, which neither of them could afford. "Yes, Master Torstan." Ben attempted a military salute, but he just ended up smacking his hand into his forehead and hoping it wouldn't leave a bruise.

"And stay away from Miss Burke. If Sir William knew you were courting her, he'd dismiss us before you can wink."

"I'm not courting her!" Ben replied hotly.

"Tell that to Sir William, if he sees you, but I doubt it will save you. Miss Burke is as high above you as the moon and stars, and nigh as untouchable, too. A word or a smile shared with her could cost us our passage to the Colony. No woman, no matter how comely or how lively her conversation, is worth losing your future for."

There was a darkness in his brother's eyes that made Ben shiver.

"There'll be women aplenty in the

Colony waiting for a well-to-do farmer, you just wait and see, Ben. You'll have your pick of them. All we need is to get there." Torstan made shooing motions. "Now, get to that gargoyle."

As Ben trudged down the hill to return to his work, he couldn't help but think that no matter how many women there were in the Colony, willing and ready for him, none of them could possibly match the kind of conversation he could have with Miss Pamela Burke.

He knew she was far too good for the likes of him – she'd likely marry some rich lord who'd take her to Italy on their honeymoon, and pay for some Italian master to capture her beauty on a canvas in oil paints too costly for Ben to afford – but it didn't stop him dreaming of the impossible. That by some miracle, the Queen would grant him lands and a title to go with it, so that he might be a suitable husband for someone as perfect as Miss Pamela Burke.

Ben laughed softly to himself. He was as likely to touch the stars as Pamela's soft, white skin. He cursed the fate that set them so close, and yet so far apart.

ELEVEN

"How goes the construction?"

Torstan almost fell off his ladder at Sir William's words, for the voice could belong to no one else.

"Ffffine, sir," Torstan said. "We are right on schedule to finish up in a fortnight, I believe. I have only the tower to complete, and my brother is working on the final gargoyle now."

Ben was indeed hammering away at a block of stone, and for once, Miss Burke was nowhere to be seen. Thank God and all his angels for that. Women were trouble, turning normally sane men into gibbering lunatics, who'd forget all their own hopes and dreams for a chance to slip between a woman's thighs. And that was only the beginning, for once you'd bedded her, there was always the chance that she'd get with child, and you'd have the girl's whole family after your head if you did not marry the wench. A girl had tried to trick him into such a marriage, but he'd managed to put her off for long enough to realise that she did not carry a child, let alone one belonging to him, and he'd had a happy escape. He would not be such a gullible fool again. He'd not bed another girl until he was certain she would make him a wonderful wife, and even then, he would not bed her until she was his wife. And he would not even consider looking for a wife until he'd built a farmhouse for them to live in, on their own land in the Swan River Colony.

Sir William seemed to be looking at him expectantly. Curses, had he asked a question while Torstan was wool-gathering?

"Forgive me, sir, but could you please repeat that?"

"If you will be finished by Saturday fortnight, I will offer you and your brother a small bonus. I am having guests to visit, you see, and I want my estate looking as prosperous as possible. If all goes well, I hope to have my daughter engaged to be married before my guests depart, if he does not choose to marry her right away, of course. So I need this folly finished as quickly as possible."

Miss Burke getting married was the best possible news. Her husband would make sure she had no time to make trouble for Ben, and there'd be more coin in it for the both of them. "Sir William, I promise you, we shall have your folly finished by sundown on Saturday fortnight. Complete with two gargoyles on the tower, as we agreed."

Sir William grunted something that sounded like "good" before he strode off toward the manor house he called Burke Castle.

TWELVE

Pamela did not return that day, nor the next, and as rain set in, further dampening Ben's mood, he despaired of seeing her again before their work was done. The only thing buoying his spirits up was working with stone, for the gargoyle had finally come to him, and he was busy chiselling it out. Unlike the first one, which was poised to strike from above, with its wings unfurled, this one sat on its small plinth, wings folded behind it, watching the world below. Ben had finished everything but its face, for he did not know what sort of expression to give it. Was it wistful, watching a world it could not be part of, or was it wearing a baleful glare at all that was wrong with the world?

"With that expression on your face, I'm beginning to wonder if you've swapped souls with a demon. Him in your body, and your soul in the stone."

"Miss Pamela!" Ben whirled around, arms wide as if he might hug her. Heavens, what was wrong with him?

Luckily, she did not seem alarmed,

merely taking a step back as she shook her head and held out her sketchbook. She'd drawn a page full of faces, all his, wearing a range of fierce, angry expressions. In one, she'd even caught him baring his teeth like a rabid beast.

He tapped the toothy one. "Can you hold this up? I think I've found the perfect face to put on this gargoyle."

Pamela only laughed harder. "No, you can't! Then I truly won't know the difference between man and demon!"

"Of course you will. I would never look at you like that."

"Indeed you should not, for I will draw a dozen pictures of your face with your eyebrows drawn low, your lip curled in a snarl, that thing you do when you flare your nostrils like a horse…"

"I do not!"

"You most certainly do! Look, Ben, you're doing it here!"

Hell and damnation, she was right. He did look like a disgruntled horse.

Slowly, his lips curled into a smile. "Forgive me, Miss Pamela, for of course you're right, as always. But I could never be angry at you."

"You might be, if you knew why I've stayed away these last few days. My father is having guests, and Burke Castle needed cleaning from top to bottom, and he said I must supervise, being the lady of the house and all, for his guests will think poorly of me if anything is amiss. I don't see why, for Mrs Jewkes, the housekeeper, saw to everything, including hiring some girls from the village to do the heavy work. She'd order them to do this and do that and put this here and that there, then ask me if I thought things were in the right place, or clean enough or…oh, a million interminable questions about nothing at all, as if I would know the best way to polish a table! Not that my answers mattered, for she directed the girls as she pleased. Now the work is done, and she's busy cooking all manner of pies and cakes for when Father's guests arrive, so I escaped." She looked particularly pleased with herself.

No, he was hardly angry. The uppermost emotion in Ben's mind was relief at seeing her again. "Escaped to help me finish the face of this demon."

They both laughed, before Ben went

back to work on the gargoyle, with frequent glances at Pamela's sketchbook.

"What was the name of the colony you plan to emigrate to?" Pamela asked.

"The Swan River Colony, on the west coast of Australia," Ben replied. "My uncle went there when he was not much older than I am now, and he sent our father a letter filled with such praise for the place, urging him to come and join him. My oldest brother, Dunstan, had just been born then, or maybe it was Torstan. Anyway, Father sent a letter back to him, telling him we'd all come to the Colony when the boys were old enough, trained in trades that would be useful in a young colony. That's why Torstan became a stonemason, and Dunstan learned to farm before he went to sea, and I…well, I just help my brother, mostly, which is what I'll do when we get there, I'm sure. Dunstan wants a farm, bigger than the one we ran here before all the landlords turned to crofting. Something to leave to his sons, if he has them. Torstan wants to build the Colony's first city, buildings that will last through the centuries. They're all about leaving legacies, my brothers are."

"What do you want to do in the colonies?" Pamela asked.

Ben shrugged. "I mean to make my fortune, one way or another. Whether it's helping my brothers with their work, or making statues of the governor and famous explorers."

"You might find gold, and strike it rich!" she said.

Ben laughed. "No, the gold rush is in the Americas, I'm sure of it. You have your colonies mixed up."

Pamela shook her head. "Father has the newspapers sent from London. Only last week, there was a story about gold in the colony of New South Wales, and in a new colony named after our Queen, Victoria. A ship full of gold arrived in England, and the papers are full of rumours that there's gold all over the entire continent of Australia. The didn't say anything about Swan River, but if it's part of the same continent, I'm sure there's gold there, too."

"Maybe," he said, not daring to hope. First he had to finish this gargoyle before he could get there, and help his brothers to establish their businesses, before he could even think of chasing after gold.

"What's this Swan River Colony like? Is it full of convicts, like New South Wales and Van Diemen's Land?"

Ben laughed. "No, it is a free colony, though many of the first settlers were indentured servants, or, like my Uncle Stanley, they signed up for a group settlement scheme. Some nobleman named Peel put up the money for ships and supplies, and brings over the men to clear the land and build houses on it, and the men get their choice of house and land when it's all done. There, we will be our own masters in a land with no lords, where we'll be lords of all we survey, free to marry whoever we wish and raise a family without fear of it all being taken away by some faraway landlord to settle his gambling debts in London."

Pamela had closed her eyes, a look of longing on her face. "Oh, I wish I could go there. It sounds like absolute bliss."

"You should. Ask your father to bring you."

"My father would never agree."

"Well, your father already has a title and lands here. He hardly needs more, especially so far away from home."

Pamela bowed her head. "Perhaps."

"I have a book my uncle left. It's old and maybe a little out of date, but it describes the Swan River Colony in great detail, if you'd like to borrow it. Perhaps you can even show your father." He paused, debating whether to run to get it now. No, better to finish this gargoyle first. "I'll bring it with me from the cottage tomorrow."

"Or I could come with you to fetch it when you finish work for the day. I don't even know where you live."

"Kelp Cottage, down by the sea. Your father let us stay there as long as we're working on the folly, but we had to fix the roof first. It had completely fallen in."

Pamela nodded. "I know where that is. It used to be one of my favourite walks on fine days, except when there is a storm and the beach is full of kelp."

"Kelp is the best fertiliser for the fields here. Without kelp, most of the farms here would not exist."

"I…know little about farming, or fertiliser, I'm afraid."

And why would she? Fine lady that

she was, Pamela would never need to work a day in her life. Too fine a lady for the likes of him.

Unless he found a fortune in gold in the Colony…

THIRTEEN

When Pamela returned home, she found her father in his library, staring at the papers on his desk with the most frightening look on his face. A mixture of fear and anger and something like desperation, edged with resignation. She had no desire to sketch this expression –

she'd much rather prefer to forget she'd ever seen it.

"Father, what is wrong?"

He looked up, weariness slumping his shoulders. "I fear that soon after our guests arrive, I shall have to go to London on business."

"I could go with you," she said, her offer only half-hearted, for she knew what he'd say.

"No, no. My lodgings are not fit for anyone but an old bachelor like me. Besides, you will have to entertain our guests. If he…if they find you pleasing, as I'm sure he will, you'll have a future better than any I could provide you with. And you will be safe. You must stay here."

"Yes, Father."

"Heaven knows someone must protect

you from my creditors, for I cannot." He said this in a voice so low, Pamela suspected she wasn't supposed to hear it.

She knew she should pretend that she hadn't heard, but the despair in her father's eyes was so heart-wrenching, she could not stay silent. "Father, if it's because of Grandfather's debts, perhaps we should rent out Burke Castle, and go to one of the Colonies. Fortunes can be made there, 'tis said, and there is gold…perhaps even enough to settle the debts against the property, and allow us to live comfortably once more."

Father stared at her for a long moment, as if he longed to do as she asked. Then he shook his head. "Migrating to the Colonies costs coin I no longer have." He picked up a bag that jingled when he shook it. "This is all I have left, after hiring servants and buying provisions to keep our guests in the style to which they are accustomed. This is the payment for the stonemasons, who are building the folly overlooking the sea. After this, I shall not have two coins to rub together, let alone pay for passage to the other side of the world, or the supplies one would need to set up a comfortable home in one of the Colonies. As for gold…I could never go grubbing in the earth like some coal miner. I am a knight of the realm, not some commoner. And you…the wilds of California are no place for a gently bred young woman. Perhaps if you were married, and travelled with your husband, it would be different, but Colbrand has his duties here at home. No, we shall take our chances here, such as they are."

Pamela's heart sank. "Perhaps not California. There is gold in Australia, too, as we read in the papers only this week."

Father shook his head. "A country filled with convicts? I should not know a day's peace, for you would not be safe, and I am but one man - I could not protect you against so many base men. No, Pamela, we must face reality, and not chase daydreams. Instead, focus all your energies on being the most charming hostess our guests have ever seen. Perhaps show them some of your prettiest sketches of the landscapes hereabouts. For if you are not enough to tempt him, perhaps the land that is your dowry might..." He reached for the decanter on the desk and poured himself a glass of whatever the strong spirits were that swam inside, then drank it down.

If Father was talking such nonsense now, it likely wasn't his first glass, nor his second or third, either. Ben's book would not change his mind, but perhaps she could read it tonight, and it would give her some ideas on how she might convince her father on the morrow.

FOURTEEN

Torstan stepped into the cottage, his face wreathed in smiles. "Set the table for three, Ben, for I have a surprise for you — the bearer of the best news you shall hear all week...nay, all year!"

Ben's mind whirled with possibilities, but it stopped dead at the sight of the man who stepped through the door after Torstan. "Dunstan…as I live and breathe, have you come home?"

Dunstan enveloped him in a hug, which didn't feel quite as encompassing as it had when he was younger. Ben was a man grown now, and not a boy any longer.

"I am only here for a brief visit, for we put to sea again soon enough. And, God willing, when I go, so shall you, for I bring good news!"

Torstan served up the bread and stew he'd brought from the village inn, while Dunstan told them how he'd arranged for them to work their passage on the *Scindian* all the way to the Swan River Colony. The coin they saved could be spent on supplies they could sell or use once they reached their destination, the better to make their way in the new world waiting for them.

"We must finish this folly first, and collect our pay, and then we may go. Will there be enough time?" Torstan asked.

"The *Scindian* will be a few weeks in port, and Captain Cammell knows I am coming, so we should be in time. But Ben must pay the Queen a visit before we go. We made a promise to Mother before she died."

Ben laughed aloud, though his brothers both looked deadly serious. "Queen Victoria would never see the likes of me!"

"Bah, not the English queen. The witch queen, who sees the future. The Queen of the Kelpies, in her cottage on the Isle of Skye." Dunstan set down his empty bowl. "I shall make all the necessary arrangements, while you finish your stonework. We shall speak to the Queen, before we depart these shores forever." He raised his cup of ale, and both Ben and Torstan followed suit. "To a new life in the new world!"

Ben echoed his toast, though a curl of trepidation tightened in his belly. He wasn't sure if it was because they were visiting a witch, leaving home, or that Pamela wouldn't be coming with them. Whatever it was, he feared their new life would not be as easy as Dunstan thought.

FIFTEEN

"Oh, look, Father, it's almost like they're about to swoop down and carry someone off!" Pamela said, pointing at the gargoyles.

Ben suppressed a smile. Yesterday, as they'd hoisted the gargoyles up to their place on top of the tower, she'd said they looked like they wanted to spit on anyone walking below. Of course, with her father here, she was every inch a lady again.

"I assure you, Miss Burke, and Sir William, that those gargoyles are fixed to the wall as firmly as the stones themselves, and even if they were to come to life, instead of just being lifelike statues, thanks to my brother Ben's carving skills, they would never be able to break free," Torstan said. "You have nothing to fear from them, Miss Burke."

"That is most reassuring, Mr Stone. To think your skills could thwart even the supernatural," Pamela said.

Ben fought not to laugh. She was making fun of Torstan, who was too nervous to notice.

Sir William frowned at his daughter. "You must forgive my daughter, Mr Stone. She has a terribly vivid imagination. It comes from reading too many novels in her younger years, I am sure, but now she is a woman grown, and soon to have a woman's responsibilities, she will have far more important things to occupy her time."

"There is nothing to forgive, Sir William. I'm sure it is a compliment to my brother that his work can stir such a lady's imagination, for I'm sure she's everything you could want in a daughter." Torstan was babbling now, even more nervous than ever. If only Sir William would just hand over their payment and go back to his castle, it would be fine.

"Indeed she is. She will make some gentleman a fine wife one day."

Torstan mumbled something that sounded vaguely supportive, but Sir William did not seem to have heard. Instead, Sir William had fixed his gaze on a horseman heading toward his home, his red Inverness coat flying behind him like a bloodied banner.

Sir William's face paled until it matched the sickly grey of the stone gargoyles. Whoever the rider was, he could not be bringing good news. He thrust a jingling bag at Torstan. "Here, your payment, as promised."

Torstan tucked it into the inner pocket of his coat, and bowed. "My thanks, Sir William. Should you ever need the services of a stonemason again, Stone brothers will be at your service."

But once again, Sir William wasn't listening. Likely because the rider had spotted them, and was now headed this way.

"Ho, Sir William! What a surprise to find you here, and not on your way to London! Did you not receive my letter?" the rider asked, reining in his horse a little too close for comfort, particularly as the beast's rolling eyes and shivering, foam-slicked sides indicated that there was no love lost between horse and rider.

Sir William eyed the horse and took several steps backward. "It arrived only yesterday, Brandon, and as I had urgent business to attend to here before making the long trip down to London, it will be a week or perhaps even two before I can even think to leave."

Pamela frowned, then ducked her head to hide her face. From her father, or Mr Brandon? Ben couldn't be sure, though he suspected the latter. Something didn't sit right about this man who abused his horse so abominably.

Brandon smiled, or at least he seemed to. He bared his teeth, curling his lips upward, but the cold expression in his eyes never changed. It was most chilling, as though watching a shark dressed in human clothes. "Urgent business, of course. I suspected it might be something like that, so I decided to travel to Burke Castle myself, to make sure you got the message."

Sir William paled further, something

Ben hadn't thought possible. "So very…kind of you, Brandon. And, having come so far, you must stay with us."

That predatory grin widened. "I wouldn't dream of doing otherwise. I have heard so much about Burke Castle, and your daughter. Perhaps she would be willing to give me a tour of the grounds?" He held his hand out to Pamela, as though he intended to pull her into the saddle with him.

Pamela ducked her head and curtseyed low, her skirts pooling on the grass around her, the picture of propriety. Except that Ben could see her face, red with anger, as she gritted her teeth to keep from replying in kind to Brandon's insult. Expecting her to sit astride a horse, close to a man she did not know, who had not even dismounted to allow a proper introduction – Ben might not be a gentleman, but he had better manners than to treat her so.

"My daughter has little taste for riding, for she rarely strays far from home. If you wish to tour the grounds, I'll have one of my grooms saddle my horse, and I shall accompany you. There are many beautiful sights to be seen," Sir William said, with a decidedly forced smile.

"Very good. But she will join us for dinner, will she not?" Brandon asked.

"Of course. She has no other engagements this evening. Pamela, see that you are home well in time for dinner, and dressed in your best," Sir William said. He coughed.

Brandon looked like the cat who'd been handed the cream. "Oh yes. Miss Pamela should be home well before dark. There is no telling what dangers lurk in the dark of a country lane."

Sir William swallowed. "Er, yes. Will you accompany me to the house? I need to…a horse. I need a horse."

A gentleman would have dismounted to walk alongside Sir William, but Brandon gave his horse a vicious kick in its side before galloping off toward Burke Castle, while Sir William hurried to catch up.

SIXTEEN

Pamela didn't trust herself to say a word in the face of Mr Brandon's rudeness, but her silence took every whit of her self control. When he and her father had finally vanished from sight, she sank down onto the Sleeping Lady's plinth and buried her head in her hands.

"Pamela? Are you all right?" Ben, bless him.

"Yes…no…I don't know anymore. I fear I am on the edge of a great precipice, and yet I cannot see what is below until I step forward, but then it will be too late, for I will already be falling…" Pamela shook her head. Perhaps her father was right. She'd read too many novels, and now they were driving her mad. What other explanation was there?

"Who is Mr Brandon? Your father seemed terribly afraid of him, though he is no gentleman, despite his fine clothes."

Discretion screamed at her not to tell him, but she'd kept her father's secrets for too long. Besides, Brandon himself might tell the whole neighbourhood, with no care for her father's reputation or her own. So Pamela let it all spill out. The enormous debts her father had inherited with Burke Castle, his attempts to remedy matters and pay things back, selling anything he had of value, even letting the servants go when he could no longer afford their wages. Yet the debts kept mounting…

"Mr Brandon is the chief of my father's creditors. Father owes him a great deal of money, and while I do not know the particulars, he has threatened my father on numerous occasions, so that Father never mentions his name except to compare him to the devil himself. Father usually visits him in London, but Mr Brandon came to Burke once, when I was very small. He only stayed one night, and left after a flaming row with my father the next morning. Two of the maids had evidently upset him, too, or so my father said – we still had maids back then. I remember Mr Brandon saying they deserved worse than a beating for their insolence. One of the girls could scarcely walk, and the other…her face swelled up something fierce, so I could hardly recognise her, what with all the bruising and all." Thank the heavens they had no maids to displease him this time. The village girls went home at night, and Mrs Jewkes was so very dependable, she would take care of Mr Brandon so well he couldn't have any complaint to make.

Ben listened to all of this, nodding his head, but saying nothing. Until his expression grew dark at the mention of the insolent maids. "My father always said never to trust a man who mistreated his horse, or beat a woman. Your Mr Brandon sounds like a villain indeed. You must be sure to lock your bedroom door at night, and be careful never to be alone with him, for that man is one of the worst villains I've ever met, I'd stake my life on it."

"He's a very wealthy man, Ben, perhaps one of the richest men in England, or so my father says. We must never speak ill of him, for he has spies everywhere, and it is only by his good graces that my father keeps himself out of debtor's prison."

Ben grimaced. "Pamela, I've only known the man for a matter of minutes, and I can already tell you, Mr Brandon has no good graces. He is as merciful as a shark in a frock coat. I would not trust him with the contents of your chamber pot, let alone allow him into my home. What your father must be thinking…but fear can turn a mind to madness as surely as a blow to the head. Perhaps you father is not thinking clearly. But you…with your quick mind, you must know better. If Mr Brandon says or does anything that makes you believe you're in danger, as I believe you are, don't stay under the same roof for a moment longer. Come to Kelp Cottage, and my brothers and I will protect you. I promise."

Pamela burst out laughing. "Ben, no. You're talking nonsense. After he's had a few glasses of brandy, men say many foolish things that turn out to be nothing in the light of day. Besides, if it's as you say, and he's not a gentleman, then his manners will be rougher than I am accustomed to, and as a good hostess, it is my role to put him at his ease, instead of taking offence. You must understand…"

Ben seized her arms, his hands searing hot even through the fabric of her sleeves. "Pamela, please, listen to me. That man is a brute and he means every insult, every slight. I know his kind and do not trust him. Promise me that if something feels wrong, if you experience even the slightest twinge of fear at something Mr Brandon says or does, you don't pause – you run. Run all the way to Kelp Cottage."

She stared into his eyes, unable to look away. Sincerity blazed out of those grey-green depths, as the heat of his hands spread up her arms and across her chest, pooling in the very heart of her. She wished she had the courage of one of the heroines of her novels, so that she might lean forward and kiss him. But she didn't dare.

"I…and my brothers…will protect you with our lives," Ben promised.

She believed him. "Thank you," she said softly. "I'm sure it won't be necessary. But thank you, all the same." The sound of hoofbeats drew her attention, as Mr Brandon and her father set off on their tour of the estate. For a moment, she thought Brandon was staring right at her, but his eyes must have been on the castle instead.

She shook herself. This was silly. She had to head home and dress for dinner, or her father would be cross. "Thank you for everything, Ben. When I bring my sketchbook out here in the morning to draw the dawn over the finished folly, you will see how silly such suspicions can be, and we may laugh about them together."

Ben's smile was darker, sadder than usual. "I hope you are right, Miss Pamela." He bowed low, before heading down the hill, toward his home.

SEVENTEEN

When he returned to the cottage, he found his brothers busy packing their things, and they greeted him with a command to do the same.

"What's going on?" he asked, shoving his spare shirts and socks into his winter cloak, before rolling it all up into a bundle and stuffing it into a sack. "Where are we going?"

"To the Swan River Colony, of course! But first we must visit the Queen of the Kelpies. I've made arrangements to borrow a boat, but we must leave tonight, and be back by Sunday night, for it'll be needed for the early morning tide on Monday," Dunstan said. "Once we return, we'll have to head out right away, if we're to reach the *Scindian* before she sails. So pack your things now, for there'll be no time otherwise."

"But...Pamela..." Ben began. He'd told her to come to them if she needed help. What if she came to their house, and they weren't home? He'd given her his word!

"We gave you time to say your goodbyes, and you took your time about it, too. Best for everyone, seeing as she'll be marrying some friend of her father's soon, or so he says."

"Not Brandon!" Ben blurted out.

Torstan shook his head. "No, someone named Colbrand, or some such thing. A widower with children, looking to give the little things another mother. A friend of his. Due to arrive tomorrow with his mother and the children. A gentleman, like a lady deserves. They'll be wed within the week, Sir William said."

Had Pamela known of this? Surely she would have said something if she had. Heaven knew they'd discussed almost every other topic under the sun. Ben swallowed. He'd known she was too good for him, and she likely hadn't said anything because she'd meant to put him at his ease, much like she planned to do with that brigand Brandon. She deserved a life as a gentleman's wife, with more servants than the lone housekeeper her father kept. This was for the best, he told himself.

Yet as he followed his brothers out into the boat and they left the shore, a chill wind whistled through his heart, whispering that he was a fool for wanting Pamela for himself, when she would never choose someone as lowly as him.

Perhaps the wind, and his brothers, were right. But that didn't make the pain at losing her any less.

EIGHTEEN

Despite Ben's warnings, dinner was a dull affair. Brandon ate like a gentleman, discussing the weather and the harvest with her father like this was a normal dinner party. That she and her father barely ate a bite between them, or that her father drank several more glasses of wine than his usual wont, seemed to go unnoticed by their guest. Nor did Mr Brandon seem to mind that Pamela said nothing at all, though his eyes lingered on her for much of the dinner, even when he spoke to her father.

Finally, dessert was done and Mrs Jewkes brought out the brandy. Pamela leaped to her feet. "I'll go see that there are coffee and cakes in the drawing room, for when you're done," she said, hurrying out.

Of course, she went to freshen up first, and in her bedchamber, she caught sight of her copy of *The Emigrant's Guide* that Ben had loaned her. She should bring it down to show Father, and perhaps he would change his mind about going to the Colonies. Perhaps Mr

Brandon, as father's biggest creditor, might support her, for surely he wanted Father's debts paid off as much as she did.

Pamela ran down the stairs, then slowed her step to something more ladylike as she passed the dining room on her way to the drawing room. The door was ajar, and the sound of raised voices spilled out.

"I tell you, Burke, there is only one way things will go, and it is how I say they will."

"But Brandon, she is betrothed to Colbrand, who will be here on the morrow with his two motherless children to celebrate their marriage! I can't break the engagement — he'll sue me for breach of contract!"

"That is why I must have her today. Tonight, in fact, my first night in my new castle. For I know what you're up to, and your father would turn over in his grave if he knew how dishonourably you mean to defraud me of what you owe! The castle and lands are mine, though they will by no means cover the cost of your debt, and if the law ties them up as your daughter's dowry, as your only heir, then you must give me the girl as well. Perhaps I shall put her to work in one of my pleasure houses. She'll fetch a pretty penny for the first year or two, until her looks fade or she catches the pox. Even then, there'll be plenty of men who'll pay extra to bed a lady."

Pamela dropped the book in horror. Luckily, it scarcely made a sound as it landed on the rug. She scooped it up again, clutching it to her chest, as if it might help to close over the chasm that had suddenly opened up there at her father's betrayal. But no...he couldn't. He wouldn't...

"Brandon, please, I beg you! She's my only daughter. She's all I have. Take the castle, and all my lands, but let her marry Colbrand. She does not deserve such a fate."

"It's all or nothing, Burke. Either you give her to me, or I shall send you both to a debtor's prison. Either way, she'll be little more than a common whore. Then again, she's likely been whoring for some time already, letting those common stone cutters have her."

"Pamela would never...she's a good

girl, she wouldn't…"

"How about we strip her naked on this very table, and see? I can easily tell whether she is a virgin or a whore, for the difference between the two is pounds and pennies, in what a man will pay for her. Send for the girl now, Burke, and you shall see her squirm!"

Ben was right.

Pamela did not stop to think. She bolted for the door.

NINETEEN

They'd taken turns rowing half the night, letting the bright moonlight light their way, then sleeping on the beach until dawn, when they headed up the hill to the cottage Dunstan swore belonged to the Queen of the Kelpies. It looked no grander than Kelp Cottage, certainly not the home of a queen, but even as Ben opened his mouth to say so, Dunstan hushed him.

"The Queen of the Kelpies has a palace beneath the water, that only kelpies can reach. She only leaves it when she grants an audience to one of us normal folk, and this is the cottage she comes to, for the other kelpies would eat us alive for daring to enter her palace. She can tell the future, and her visions come true. Mum said she was told she'd have three boys, who'd journey across the sea and live in a country so strange that white was black, and it wasn't until she read Uncle Stanley's letter about swans being black instead of white that she understood. The Queen made Mum swear she would send all three of us to her to hear our futures told, and it was Mum's dying wish that we come here today." Dunstan looked around at the others. "So we will bow down to the Queen, thank her most graciously for granting Mum and us this gift, and listen to every word she has to say."

Ben nodded. He wanted to believe that this woman could tell him his future, but only if it was a future he wanted. If it wasn't…then he'd rather not hear it at all.

Dunstan knocked at the cottage door. It swung open.

"Enter," said a voice from inside.

Dunstan went in first, and Ben came last, pulling the door shut behind him. It took him a moment for his eyes to adjust to the darkness inside, but when they did, he let out a gasp.

The cottage was built in the lee of a cliff, overlooking a pretty lake, but where Ben expected see the rear wall of the cottage, there was no wall at all. The cottage stretched deep inside the cliff, where the space opened up into a throne room worthy of Queen Victoria herself. At the back of this long hall, on a dais lit by torches that burned blue, a woman in black sat on a throne. It wasn't until they approached the foot of the dais that Ben realised the throne wasn't gold or silver, but made of bone-white driftwood and woven kelp. The Queen's crown matched her throne, a nest of white driftwood spikes woven together with kelp, which glowed eerily atop her dark hair.

Dunstan bowed low, gesturing for the others to do the same. "Thank you for seeing us, Your Majesty. Our mother, Marisa Muir, before she married our father, Alan Stone, and became Marisa Stone, charged us with visiting you before we depart our home shores. She brought me to you many years ago, before I went to sea, and now that she is gone, I bring my brothers to you, on the eve of our departure for the Swan River Colony. We ask but one question, as our mother bade us: what does our future hold?"

The Queen shifted in her seat, leaning forward as she made an imperious gesture with her hand. "Get up. This is not the English court, where bowing and scraping is expected. My people stand tall, like the men they are, and though you are not kelpies, if you are true sons of Marisa Muir, then your hearts are with my people. So, tell me, Torstan Stone…do you have the heart of a kelpie?"

When Torstan didn't answer, she turned to Ben. "Young Ben, what about you? Do you have the heart of a kelpie?"

Ben wet his lips. "I've never met a kelpie before, and I don't know any well enough to know the secrets of their heart. Truth be told, I'm not sure I even know my own heart, for it wants to pull me in many directions all at once."

The Queen nodded. "So I see, and yet your future is clearer than either of your brothers'. Did you know that your mother did me a great service?"

Ben shook his head. Maybe his brothers had heard the story from Mum, but he'd been too little to remember.

"When I was a young wife, many years ago now, my husband beat me, accusing me of barrenness. One day, he beat me so badly, I thought I would die, and he carried my body to the shore of the loch, as an offering for the kelpies, for I was no use for anything else, or so he said. Marisa, who was just a girl then, heard the fight and saw him leave the house with what she thought was my dead body, and she followed him. She hid in the bushes until he'd left me, and when she discovered I was still alive, she tended to my wounds. It was a summer night, much like last night, with a bright moon in the sky. I'd heard the tales of the kelpies, and how they loved the taste of human flesh, and I urged her over and over to leave me to my fate, to save herself.

"But Marisa never left.

"Before dawn they came, silently sliding from the water, a mix of horses and men, or so I thought. I was struck speechless with terror, but your mother stood up, folded her arms across her chest, and told them what had happened to me. How my husband beat me and left me for dead, or to be devoured.

"Then she issued her challenge. She asked them if they were beasts of burden, doing the bidding of brutes who would do this to a woman, or were they protectors, more than men, who would see justice done?"

The Queen laughed, rocking a little on her throne at the memory.

Then she continued, "It wasn't until later that I discovered one of the horse kelpies was her brother, a man I thought I'd known all my life, and that they had no intention of harming her or me. Have you heard the tales of the kelpies, Ben Stone?"

"They're water horses that live in the lochs, which can take the form of men or horses, to seduce maidens into the water where they devour them, leaving nothing but their entrails on the shore," Ben said. "At least, that's what the stories say."

The Queen nodded. "Ah, the stories men tell. Don't go down to the loch, or the kelpies might eat you. But the women who know them, who know the secrets of their hearts, tell a different tale. A tale told in darkness, and in pain, and only to those who need to know. Women like I was that night on the shore. Women who want to disappear, so no one will come searching, or hurt them again. While they live out their lives with their chosen kelpie husbands, protected and cherished, as they should be."

"Is that what you did?" Ben asked.

"Ben!" Dunstan hissed.

"Uh, Your Majesty," Ben added, ducking his head.

"No, Ben, I did not disappear. Instead, it was my husband who went missing. On his way home from the tavern, he stumbled into the loch and drowned. His body washed up on the same shore where he'd left me, and I became a widow, and the owner of his farm by the loch. But I was not a widow for long, for I had caught the eye of the King of the Kelpies, and he had caught mine in return. And what my late husband would be horrified to learn, if he knew, was that when I recovered from that last beating, months after his death, for bones take time to heal…was that I could see the future. Visions of what will come, if you continue to follow the same path. And that is why they named me their queen, though the king I loved is king no longer, and a new kelpie wears his crown now, as is proper."

"I am sorry for your loss, Your Majesty," Dunstan said softly.

The Queen laughed. "The king's crown is no loss. Most kings do not wear it for more than a few years, before they hold an election for a new king so that they may pass it on. Kingship is a heavy burden, and I would not wish it on anyone. My husband stepped down on the day they crowned me, and we have not regretted a single day together. We still have many more to come, too."

Dunstan blinked. For once, he looked lost for words.

Ben cleared his throat. "So what is the secret in the heart of a kelpie, Your Majesty?"

The Queen smiled down on him. "Love. The desire to protect, to nurture all that we hold dear. And if you are truly Marisa's sons, then you have her heart.

The heart of a kelpie. Protectors, all three of you, who will love fiercely and do all that you must for the women you love."

Pamela. He'd be able to protect Pamela from her father's evil creditor. Ben breathed out a sigh of relief.

"Do you wish to know what your future holds, Ben Stone?" the Queen asked, as if she'd heard his thoughts. Perhaps she had.

"Yes, Your Majesty," he replied. He hoped he wouldn't regret it.

"Then listen well."

TWENTY

The swiftest way out of the house was through the tradesmen's entrance, at the bottom of the servants' stairs, and that's where Pamela went, running through the kitchen, past a startled Mrs Jewkes, before flinging open the door and flying out into the night. Across the vegetable garden, through the garden gate, then out into the field where the horses spent their days. Dewy grass crunched beneath her evening slippers, soaking through both the shoes and her stockings, but still she ran.

As she approached the clifftop path that led to Kelp Cottage, Pamela wished she'd thought to bring a lantern. Falling off the cliff to the rocks below might be preferable to the fate Brandon had in mind for her, but Pamela was no gothic romance heroine – she'd rather live than meet a tragic end.

The path ahead sparkled suddenly in a ray of moonlight, as that ghostly orb appeared through the wispy clouds to light her way. The cliff edge was closer than she'd thought. A few more steps and she might have gone over. She slowed, picking her way carefully along the path, until she saw the fork that led down to the beach. The descent was darker here, in the lee of the cliffs, and she nearly turned her ankle on unseen rocks, but she made it to the beach. There was no path to follow now, just the wide road that was the rocky beach, edged by dark cliffs on one side and shimmering moonlit waves on the other.

Kelp Cottage loomed like a crouching monster on the headland at the end of the beach, and she had to scramble up the steep path to reach it. She thought she heard the sound of ripping cloth as her skirt caught on something, but her clothes were of no consequence now, as she kept going up to the safety Ben had promised.

For all that she didn't trust Brandon, or even her father, she knew she could rely on Ben. He'd given her his word, and no man of honour went back on his word. She would be safe. He'd promised.

The cottage windows were dark, but the door opened easily at her touch. Darkness yawned before her, with not even a fire to light the way, but the nights were too warm to need anything but a small cookfire, and Ben had confessed to her long ago that as neither he nor his brother could cook, they bought their food from the inn in town.

That's where they must be now, she decided, closing the door behind her. Taking dinner in the tavern, celebrating a job well done, before coming home to sleep.

A thin veil of moonlight filtered through the salt-crusted window, outlining a white box on the mantlepiece, beside a candlestick. Pamela moved in for a closer look. Lucifers! She hadn't seen Lucifer matches since her mother was alive. Her mother had insisted it was the most ladylike way to light a fire, better than risking one's hands and nails with a flint and tinder, before huffing and puffing down on one's knees like some foreign heathen to his campfire deity.

With trembling hands, Pamela drew out a match and scraped it along the side, just as her mother had in her memory. It took a few tries before the sparks caught, and the flame flared to life, but the moment she touched it to the candle wick, she had light enough to see by.

She was alone. The lantern that Ben said usually hung over the table was gone, likely to light their way to and from the tavern. They would return soon, for it must be nigh on midnight, if not later.

In the meantime, she would wait.

Pamela sank down onto a chair, suddenly more exhausted than she'd realised. If she closed her eyes for but a moment…

She jerked awake, her neck aching. How…? Oh, she'd fallen asleep in one of the cottage's hard chairs. She could not have been asleep for more than a few moments, for the candle had hardly burned down, but if the men took much longer, she could hardly stay in the chair. The bed beckoned.

She rose, tottering for a few steps before her stiffened legs woke up, and headed for the door. Best to bar it, if she was going to sleep. The men would know something was amiss when they arrived home to find their door locked, and they'd surely knock loud enough to wake her. She set the candle in the window, so that they might know someone was inside. There.

Secure in her small sanctuary, Pamela trudged to the bed. When she sat down, straw crackled in the mattress beneath her. She laughed softly. She'd never slept on a straw bed before. She slipped off her wet shoes and stockings, then decided to add her evening gown and corset to the small pile of clothes on the chair. Under the coverlet, no one would see she wore only a shift.

But sleep would not come. For even when the brothers returned, what was she to do? She could not return home, if her father meant to give her to Brandon. Yet if Father did not hand her over, he'd go to debtor's prison to work off his debts.

Moonlight streaked through the window again, landing on a book that lay on the table. *The Emigrant's Guide.* Of course! She could go with Ben and his brothers to the Swan River Colony, and perhaps find her fortune there. She'd read books about girls who dressed as boys to disguise themselves and went on adventures. She had only to…

Wear tight trousers so that all and sundry might see her legs and ankles? Not likely! It was almost as bad as going naked. No, she'd never have the courage to dress like a man. Besides, her breasts would give her away. There was no hiding those.

What had her father said? Something about how she'd be safe even in the wilds of California if she was married. In the Swan River Colony, a place where it would be safe to raise a family…

She'd have to ask Ben to marry her. Her father might object, but he'd lost all hope of controlling her fate when he'd agreed to give her to Brandon. So to hell and damnation with her father, or at the very least, debtor's prison. Even if Ben objected, they might pretend she was his wife, just as long as he brought her along. Yes. She would go to the Swan River Colony, and she and Ben and his brothers would build a future together. Far from Burke Castle and its debts, and the cruel hands of Brandon. Maybe they'd even find gold, and their fortunes would be made.

The future shone bright in her mind's eye.

Then, with a small sigh, she settled down to sleep while she waited for Ben and his brothers to return, so that together, they could make her vision a reality.

TWENTY-ONE

The Queen fixed her gaze on Ben. "Ben Stone, one day in the distant future, you will settle down to a happy life as an artist, sharing a cottage overlooking the sea with your heiress sweetheart. But between now and then you will encounter many trials on your way to this ultimately happy ending. All might seem lost, and so dark you cannot see your way through to the light on the other side, but if you keep to your current path, true to your heart, a bright future awaits you in your home across the sea."

She turned to Torstan. "Torstan Stone, your fate is much like your brother Dunstan's, which has not wavered since that first time Marisa brought him to me. Both of you will find your sweethearts halfway around the world, across the sea. You, too, will need to work hard to find the happiness I see in your future, if you but hold true to your hearts."

Her gaze swept across all three of them. "I glimpse the sparkle of gold in your future, all of you, but the vision is not yet clear, so it might not come to pass. Such is the nature of my gift. What I do know is that there is much conflict surrounding the gold, and you will need to fight, fight for each other, and the women you love, for even a hope of seeing this gold."

"Thank you, Your Majesty," Dunstan said, bowing low.

Ben struggled to rein in his whirling thoughts, as he copied Dunstan.

He would marry Pamela, and they'd be happy together. He'd be able to work as an artist, and not a mason or a farmer. It was better than he'd dared hope. And gold…if the Queen was right, they might even find gold. Such a shining future, he could almost see it himself. He couldn't wait to get home to Kelp Cottage, to tell

Pamela.

He had no memory of the long walk back to the boat, or of taking his turn at the oars to row their little boat home. The sun had tipped over the high point of noon and started slipping down the afternoon sky toward its twilight rest in the sea when they finally arrived at Kelp Cottage.

His brothers headed for the door, but Ben turned away, toward the path that led to Burke Castle. Pamela. He had to tell Pamela.

He found his way blocked by three men. One he recognised as the parish constable. The second was the village blacksmith who was easily twice as wide as Ben or either of his brothers, and the third man he thought might work at the tavern.

"Which of you are the Stone brothers?" the constable demanded.

Ben grinned. "Well, all of us. All three of us are the Stone brothers. Dunstan, Torstan and me – Ben Stone."

"Then you are under arrest, all three of you. You must come with us."

Torstan stepped up to Ben's side. "There must be some mistake. We're stonemasons, we've just finished a big building project for Sir William Burke, over at Burke Castle. Ask him. He will vouch for us. We've committed no crime."

The constable shook his head. "That's for the magistrate to decide. You must come with us."

"But just let me speak to Sir William.

He'll vouch for us, I'd stake my life on it," Ben said.

"Sir William's the one who sent for me, calling for your arrest. Now, come with us, for you're in enough trouble, and you don't want to add resisting arrest on top of the other charges."

The brothers exchanged glances. What choice did they have?

"We'll come with you," Dunstan said.

Ben cast a longing look at the path to Burke Castle, and Pamela. Things would work out, just as the Queen of the Kelpies had said, but first he had to get through this first trial.

All would be well, he swore, just as the Queen said. He knew it in his heart.

ABOUT THE AUTHOR

Demelza Carlton has always loved the ocean, but on her first snorkelling trip she found she was afraid of fish.

She has since swum with sea lions, sharks and sea cucumbers and stood on spray drenched cliffs over a seething sea as a seven-metre cyclonic swell surged in, shattering a shipwreck below.

Demelza now lives in Perth, Western Australia, the shark attack capital of the world.

The *Ocean's Gift* series was her first foray into fiction, followed by her suspense thriller *Nightmares* trilogy. She swears the *Mel Goes to Hell* series ambushed her on a crowded train and wouldn't leave her alone.

Want to know more? You can follow Demelza on Facebook, Twitter, YouTube or her website, Demelza Carlton's Place at:

www.demelzacarlton.com

More Books by Demelza Carlton

<u>**Colony: Aqua series**</u>

Halcyon (#1)

Poseidon (#2)

Apollo (#3)

<u>**Siren of Secrets series**</u>

Ocean's Secret (#1)

Ocean's Gift (#2)

Ocean's Infiltrator (#3)

<u>**Nightmares Trilogy**</u>

Nightmares of Caitlin Lockyer (#1)

Necessary Evil of Nathan Miller (#2)

Afterlife of Alana Miller (#3)

<u>**Romance Island Resort series**</u>
Maid for the Rock Star (#1)
The Rock Star's Email Order Bride (#2)
The Rock Star's Virginity (#3)
The Rock Star and the Billionaire (#4)
The Rock Star Wants A Wife (#5)
The Rock Star's Wedding (#6)
Maid for the South Pole (#7)

<u>**Romance a Medieval Fairytale series**</u>

Enchant: Beauty and the Beast Retold

Dance: Cinderella Retold

Fly: Goose Girl Retold

Revel: Twelve Dancing Princesses Retold

Silence: Little Mermaid Retold

Awaken: Sleeping Beauty Retold

Embellish: Brave Little Tailor Retold

Appease: Princess and the Pea Retold

Blow: Three Little Pigs Retold

Return: Hansel and Gretel Retold

Wish: Aladdin Retold

Melt: Snow Queen Retold

Spin: Rumpelstiltskin Retold

Kiss: Frog Prince Retold

Reflect: Snow White Retold

Roar: Goldilocks Retold

Cobble: Elves and the Shoemaker Retold

Float: Enchanted Horse Retold

Steal: Forty Thieves Retold

Call: Pied Piper Retold

Fall: Scheherazade Retold

Feather: Swan Maidens Retold

Curse: Rose Red Retold

Cross: Billy Goats Gruff Retold

Weave: Rapunzel Retold

Claim: Puss in Boots Retold